Tough Trails

Irene Morck

orca soundings

ORCA BOOK PUBLISHERS

Library and Archives Canada Cataloguing in Publication

Morck, Irene
Tough trails / Irene Morck.
(Orca soundings)
ISBN 10: 1-55143-271-4
ISBN 13: 978-1-55143-271-7

1. Horses--Juvenile fiction. I. Title. II. Series.
PS8576.O628T6 2003   jC813'.54   C2003-910686-1
PZ7.M7885To 2003

First published in the United States, 2003
Library of Congress Control Number: 2003105880

Summary: Ambrose buys an old, infirm horse to work the mountains. When a storm comes, the horse leads a young boy to safety.

Orca Book Publishers gratefully acknowledges the support for its publishing programs provided by the following agencies: the Government of Canada through the Book Publishing Industry Development Program and the Canada Council for the Arts, and the Province of British Columbia through the BC Arts Council and the Book Publishing Tax Credit.

Design by Christine Toller
Cover photography by Eyewire

ORCA BOOK PUBLISHERS
PO Box 5626, STN. B
VICTORIA, BC CANADA
V8R 6S4

ORCA BOOK PUBLISHERS
PO Box 468
CUSTER, WA USA
98240-0468

www.orcabook.com
Printed and bound in Canada.

010 09 08 07 • 6 5 4 3

This is Cora's book.
It's for Cora and Peter and Kathy, for being there to
make me want to keep writing.
It's for Mogens and my family, for everything.
But it's still Cora's book because she made me reach.

Other books by Irene Morck

A Question of Courage
Between Brothers
Tiger's New Cowboy Boots
Five Pennies: A Prairie Boy's Story
Apples and Angel Ladders:
A Collection of Pioneer Christmas Stories
Old Bird

Chapter One

I've always had to act tougher than I've felt. When you're seventeen and stuck with a name like Ambrose Virgil Metford, you have to act tough. Especially when you're working for your uncle, taking trail riders high up into Alberta's Rocky Mountains.

But I sure wasn't feeling tough as I wandered around the corrals behind the auction buildings. The auction would soon be starting. My pack horse, Blackie, had to be sold here today. He would have to be killed for meat.

This was ripping through my guts just as the sharp rock had ripped through Blackie's tendon yesterday. We'd been crossing a fast river when it happened. Blackie had screamed in pain as he collapsed in the water. In a split second my favorite horse became suitable only for dog food. He had struggled out of the river, lurching on three legs. We'd injected him full of painkiller so he could make it to the trailer and endure his last ride to town.

Now my beloved Blackie stood here, waiting for death. The meat buyers would bid hard for such a big solid horse. Then he'd be trucked away to a slaughter house.

Somehow I was supposed to quit thinking about Blackie long enough to buy a new pack horse. Today, at the auction, I had to find another animal like him — young, sensible and strong.

I shoved my hands into my pockets, then yanked one hand out as my fingers touched the roll of twenties. Uncle Mac had sent along two hundred dollars in case Blackie's selling price wasn't quite enough to buy the new horse. I knew Uncle Mac was hoping I wouldn't have to use much of this extra cash. Money was tight in the outfitting business.

"Looking for a good horse?" a tiny gray-haired lady called as I passed one of the corrals. A tall, muscular, reddish-brown mare stood beside her. But that wasn't what made me stop. It was the old lady's eyes that got to me. Those eyes — pale blue, almost glassy, so sad and trapped, yet refusing to cry.

The old lady looked as though her heart was aching as badly as mine. Still, you could see she wasn't going to break. I couldn't help but admire her.

"Even the youngest kid can ride this horse," said the lady. "My granddaughters grew up riding her. And she's harness trained . . . "

"I . . . uh, we . . . need a horse for packing in the mountains," I said. Nobody's horses looked right compared to Blackie. This one looked too old. Probably about fifteen years of age, a bit swaybacked. This horse might be sold for meat too. At auctions, so many horses go for meat.

"My mare could pack," the lady said. "This horse could do anything."

"Has she packed before?" It was hard to be interested.

"No, but she's very strong. Every day this winter she pulled the hay sled when we fed our cows. And she's sensible. My husband had a heart attack when he had her hooked to the hay wagon this spring, and this horse didn't even run away." The lady never took her eyes off mine. "We found my husband dead, but this mare hadn't moved."

"I'm sorry," I said. "About your husband."

The lady leaned her head against the mare. "This horse is all I've got left. Now she has to go too. Right from a foal, she was real easy to train. She learns fast."

Just like my Blackie, I thought. Blackie was the first foal I'd ever seen born. Five years ago, I just happened to be out in the pasture when Uncle Mac's best pack horse, Star, was giving birth. A few minutes later I had watched in amazement as Star's wet black colt struggled to stand and figured out how to walk. I had named him. I had helped Uncle Mac halter-train him. Then when Blackie was old enough, I had taught him to pack . . .

I forced myself to look back at the gray-haired lady. "How come you're selling your horse?" I asked.

"My son says I have to . . . " The woman's eyes flashed, angry. "Have to go . . . to an old folks home — this week." She spat out the words. "Leave my farm, sell my horse, move into one tiny room in Edmonton. I've never lived in a city."

I nodded. It was bad enough to live in a town. I always spent as much time as possible at Uncle Mac's farm, even before I worked for him.

The lady gulped and continued. "My

son says I can't take care of the farm. I had a stroke after my husband died. But I'm a lot better now. I just can't drive, that's all. My neighbor brought my horse and me here."

The old lady twisted the faded blue halter rope in her hands, staring across the corrals. "What if this horse . . . what if nobody . . . ?" Her voice trailed off.

I knew what she was thinking. But this horse had nothing wrong with her. She should not go for meat.

I leaned on the rail, looking at the mare. Her glossy coat showed she was healthy. She had long, straight legs and good hooves. The horse stood watching me, as though she were pleading too.

You could see this mare was getting old, though — some white hairs in her red coat, a few wrinkles above her eyes. Still, she might be able to do a couple more years of hard work. Most horses didn't get sold to a meat buyer until they were eighteen or older.

"What's your name?" the old lady asked.

Why did she have to know my name? "It's Ambrose," I answered reluctantly. "Ambrose Metford."

"Ambrose is a good name," she declared. I winced. She smiled gently as though she understood. "I'm Mrs. Longhurst." Then she pointed to the mare. "Her name is Society Girl."

Society Girl! That was worse than Ambrose. If I bought the horse, *that* name would change. A cowboy couldn't have a horse named Society Girl.

"I called her that soon after she was born," the lady said. "She wanted to be with the other horses, but she acted a bit above them, kind of cool and proud. Like a society girl."

The old lady cooed the name again. The mare put her ears forward and leaned her head against Mrs. Longhurst's shoulder. At least the horse liked *her* stupid name.

"How old is your horse?" I asked.

"Twenty-five," the woman answered, looking down for the first time.

"Twenty-five! A twenty-five-year-old horse is good only for . . . "

She glared at me. "This horse is in better shape than most horses half her age. We've always taken good care of her."

I turned to walk away. "Sorry," I said. "She'd have to be able to work hard in the mountains."

"She's always worked hard," Mrs. Longhurst shouted after me. "She would never let you down."

I walked on, stopping at several corrals to talk to people with young horses. There were quite a few animals I could bid on, including two experienced pack horses. They were being sold because their owners didn't trail-ride any more. If only somebody else could make the decision for me. Being trusted to buy just the right horse would be bad enough at the best of times.

Many corrals were full of unattended horses, milling around. Some were lame, with long, split, turned-up hooves. Some were young, obviously wild, rolling their eyes, snorting. Some were very old, stiff, hardly able to walk. Meat horses for sure, all of these. But they weren't good for anything else.

I stood in front of Blackie's pen again. Blackie hung his head over the rail as I scratched his face. He'd always loved that, right from when he was little.

I had missed him so much the last couple of summers. He'd been packing in the mountains while Uncle Mac paid me to stay behind and look after his farm.

This year I'd asked Uncle Mac to let me try working in the mountains. He said he'd have to hire somebody else then to stay on the farm, so he couldn't pay me until the end of the season. That's what made me get up the courage to ask if I could have Blackie instead of cash for my summer's wages.

To my surprise, Uncle Mac had agreed and offered to throw my favorite saddle horse Dusty in on the deal. "And," he added, "Dusty and Blackie can stay free on my farm as long as you use them for this outfit in the summers. A guy your age should work with his own saddle horse and pack horse."

Now my very own pack horse stood waiting to be sold at an auction. Blackie was full of painkiller, still hardly able to put any weight on his sliced tendon. And tomorrow he'd be gone forever.

Blackie leaned his head against my shoulder. Maybe I should have let Uncle Mac or even Janice bring him to the auction. But that would really have given Janice a chance to look down on me.

Nobody had the right to talk to me the way that scrawny blonde always did. So what if Janice had already worked for Uncle Mac three years — since she was fourteen? She still had no right to put me down all the time.

When Uncle Mac had offered to be the one to take Blackie to the auction, Janice sneered at me. "You'd have to be a total coward to desert your horse on his last trip."

"Nobody but me is taking him," I'd said.

I knew that Uncle Mac had hired Janice

because he felt sorry for her. Just because her drunk father ran off leaving her mom with six kids. So what if Janice now outpacked and outrode Uncle Mac himself? That didn't mean she should act like she was better than everyone else.

Blackie nudged my pockets, searching for oats. I could hardly look at him. Sometimes I wished I could be as tough as Janice, even though she was such a pain. Cowboys were supposed to be tough.

I glanced across the corrals to Mrs. Longhurst and her horse, standing with their heads pressed together. A man strolled by them, obviously shopping too. The old lady called to him. He stood listening, then shook his head and walked on the same way I had. He wasn't looking for an old horse either.

Quite a few people were walking around, sizing up horses before the sale. Some stopped to listen to Mrs. Longhurst, nodding at her, smiling. Maybe somebody would buy old Society Girl for their kids. She was in too good a condition to die.

A voice boomed through the loud-speaker, telling us the sale was about to begin. Sick to my stomach, I stood for a few more seconds with my arms wrapped tightly around my big strong horse's neck. Then I backed away, giving him one last rub on his forehead.

Gulping, I headed towards the main building to find a seat beside the auction ring.

Chapter Two

One of the first horses chased into the ring was a skinny blue roan mare. She kicked the wide metal door as it slammed shut behind her, then stamped around in the wood shavings. She kept on flashing her teeth and kicking out at the ring man.

A mean horse, that one. I thought the meat buyers had her for sure. But just when the auctioneer was ready to accept a bid, a red-headed girl raised her hand. Everyone turned to stare at the girl. I knew the type. She'd just have to rescue this horse. Janice always called that type of person a bleeding heart.

At $490 the meat buyers smirked and let the redhead have her horse. Maybe someone like that might buy Society Girl. Too bad there was no hope for Blackie.

When it was Blackie's turn to be chased into the ring, I could hardly look up. The meat buyers bid eagerly against each other. They got the price to $910.

The ring man cracked his whip. It felt as though that whip was cutting straight through me. I kept my head down so I didn't have to see my Blackie limp out towards the meat buyer's corral.

Rubbing my hand across my eyes, I tried to force myself to focus on the sale. Uncle Mac was depending on me to get a horse we could pack for the season. And if I wanted, the new horse could be mine at the end of the summer.

A couple of well-behaved horses were ridden in next, but I could hardly stand to look at them. Anyway, they were too slim and delicate for packing.

The entry gate clanged again. Into the ring walked the tiny gray-haired lady, leading her big red mare. The noise softened. It wasn't very often you saw an old lady in an auction ring. I wished I'd sat farther from the front so I wouldn't have to see the pain in those pale blue eyes.

The auctioneer picked up the paper Mrs. Longhurst handed him. Then he mumbled off the words. "This mare's experienced pulling sleighs and wagons. Little kids can ride her. She'll do anything for you."

The auctioneer began his loud rhythmic chant. "Who'll give me twelve hundred for this horse? Twelve. Who'll give me twelve?"

That wasn't a meat price. That was the price for a nice riding or driving horse. Maybe the auctioneer thought he could find a home for her.

I looked around. No one was bidding. "Eleven hundred. Who'll gimme eleven?" Still no one lifted a hand.

The old lady and Society Girl stood together in the center of the ring. They were motionless, their heads high. Mrs. Longhurst should be leading the mare around, even trotting her. At least that would show off how well the horse could move.

"A thousand. Nice-looking mare. She's well worth a thousand," said the auctioneer. Silence. "Nine then. Look at the muscles on that horse. A big solid animal. Gimme eight-fifty ? Eight?"

Now the meat buyers were in the game. One of them nodded, touching his finger to the brim of his hat.

"I got eight. Who'll gimme eight-twenty?" chanted the auctioneer.

I wondered if the lady knew which men were meat buyers. No, she'd have no way of knowing. Mrs. Longhurst wasn't used to going to auction sales.

The three meat buyers quickly got the

price up to $880. The old lady scuffed her thick brown shoes in the wood shavings.

She'd loved her horse since it was a foal, just as I had. With Blackie, there'd been no choice. He had to go for meat. But her strong healthy animal should not have to die too. I scanned the crowd for faces that might be interested in using a good old horse.

What about families with little kids? They probably thought this mare was too big, thought kids should have ponies. Sometimes a big horse — even one this tall — was best for a kid. Especially a horse this gentle.

The auctioneer was winding down. He was going to accept a bid. "Eight-ninety?"

One of the meat buyers, a man with a grubby old jacket, lifted his hand again. Hatred surged through me. It was the same man who had bought my Blackie.

"I've got eight-ninety," said the auctioneer. "Nine hundred?"

The old lady looked around desperately. Yes, she did know what kind of people were bidding. Her frantic, pale blue eyes met mine.

And, powerless to stop it, I felt my hand rise. Surprised, the auctioneer started the bidding again. Up we went to $920. Shrugging their shoulders, the three meat buyers sank back into their seats.

"Sold. To the young man down at ringside!"

An icy feeling overcame me as reality set in. I'd bought a horse. Mad at Mrs. Longhurst, even madder at myself, I walked slowly to the corrals. Now who was the bleeding heart?

The old lady spotted me and waved me towards her. "Thank you, Ambrose," she said. "Thank you."

I didn't answer, just nodded.

No way could I ever let Uncle Mac or Janice know this horse was twenty-five years old. Especially not Janice.

I'd pretend I didn't know Society Girl's age. That might work. Uncle Mac was good at telling a horse's age by its teeth. But after a horse was fifteen or so, no one could tell its age anymore. They get "smooth mouthed," with no rings or any other markings left as their teeth wear down.

Mrs. Longhurst stood without speaking, watching as I ran my hands over Society Girl's muscles. No fat anywhere on that horse. And Society Girl didn't look her age. Neither Uncle Mac nor Janice could ever guess. They'd better not — or I'd be in one heap of trouble.

I opened the door of Uncle Mac's horse trailer. Silent, Mrs. Longhurst stood back.

As soon as I pulled on Society Girl's halter rope, the horse jumped into the trailer.

The old lady stood watching as I started the truck. She lifted her hand, as though she were reaching out to me and to Society Girl.

No, Mrs. Longhurst wouldn't cry. But as I drove off, her thin shoulders drooped, and the life went out of her eyes.

Chapter Three

It was a long three hours' driving that after-noon to the end of the road where I'd be leaving the truck and trailer. From there it would be another few miles of riding back to Uncle Mac's base camp.

The farther I drove, the worse I felt. I hated being such a wimp. I shouldn't have let myself fall to pieces about losing Blackie.

Then I would never have been sucked into buying this ancient mare. Why did I always have to be such a sap?

Finally I reached the end of the road. Dusty and Star were still tied to the trees where I had left them that morning. They'd eaten all of their hay and emptied the water pails that I'd left hanging from their trees.

When I'd taken Blackie away in the trailer, Dusty and Star had whinnied frantically as though they knew what I was doing. Good thing Star couldn't understand what had happened to her son.

I backed Society Girl out of the trailer and tied her to a tree. She stood watching while I filled the four pack boxes. Society Girl and Star would each be carrying a pair of these boxes into camp. The pack boxes would be heavy today with the groceries I'd bought in town before the auction.

First I saddled Dusty. Then I loaded Star with her heavy pack. She stood calmly, her eyes half-closed. I'd have given anything to be packing her son Blackie next.

It worried me to think about packing this new horse. Many horses were terrified the first time they were packed. Some bucked or reared. Quite a few horses went crazy the first time the tarp was spread over the pack. Sometimes there was a wreck when a horse first felt the lash rope tighten around its body.

It was getting late. I could put the last two boxes on Dusty. He had packed before. I could just ride Society Girl to camp for now. I could train her to pack when other people were around to help in case anything went wrong.

But Uncle Mac had sent me to buy a pack horse. Janice would have plenty to say if I came into camp packing my "riding" horse and riding my new "pack" horse.

I was so mad at myself for buying this horse. Everybody knew the saying "You can't teach an old horse new tricks." So what kind of idiot would think he could teach a twenty-five-year-old horse how to pack?

Waddling with the heavy box, I headed towards Society Girl.

She stepped back.

"Stand still," I yelled.

The horse snorted.

Of course I should have stood quietly then. I should have given her time to get used to what was happening. But no, I just kept tramping towards her with that pack box, yelling louder, "Stand still!"

Society Girl moved away, her eyes filled with fear. I hated how I was acting, but feeling ashamed made me even angrier. I slammed the pack box down and grabbed the mare by the halter rope. Shouting, I yanked her head.

She pulled away, terrified.

Okay, we'll try the scariest thing right now, I thought. *Because it looks like you'll be headed back to the meat buyers.* I scooped up the tarp and stomped towards Society Girl.

She snorted.

My anger was making me stupid. I didn't care that the canvas tarp was dragging and flapping. I just kept advancing.

The mare jumped sideways.

I bellowed. Well, that did it. She leaned back on the halter rope, her body crouched, almost falling over, her eyes rolling with horror.

All of a sudden I thought of Mrs. Longhurst's desperate eyes. A wave of pain went through me. Mrs. Longhurst would die if she could see how I was treating her beloved horse.

I sat on a stump, my hands on my head. I took a deep breath. I wasn't giving this horse a fair chance. Society Girl had never known anything but kindness. My anger was going to ruin her. And Uncle Mac would have been horrified to see me treating any horse so badly.

"Society Girl," I said softly. "Society Girl."

She was listening, her ears flicking back and forth. I went to the truck, got a soft brush from behind the seat. Calling her name, I walked slowly towards the mare. She looked suspicious. But when I started to brush her, she began to relax. "I'm sorry," I said. "I'm really sorry, Society Girl." It was a good thing nobody could hear me.

I brushed her another few minutes. She seemed peaceful now, almost grateful. "Well, old girl, let's try that tarp again," I said. "It's the scariest, isn't it?"

This time I approached slowly with the tarp, talking softly. She snorted. I stood still, cooing her name as Mrs. Longhurst had done. The horse calmed right down. Just a few foot-steps at a time I brought the tarp closer. She remained motionless as I kept talking. I let her sniff the tarp. She snorted. "That's okay, Society Girl," I said. She relaxed again.

When I touched her shoulder with the tarp she jumped away. I patted her gently. "Society Girl, it's okay. It's okay, Society Girl." In minutes she let me rub her anywhere with that tarp.

"Good girl," I said. "Well, let's try this packing business again." I picked up one of the boxes and headed towards her. Her eyes widened. She remembered the pack box had come with yelling and roughness. "You'll be all right this time," I said, standing quietly with the box. "Society Girl, it's okay, Society Girl." It was amazing to see how that calmed her. It was almost as though she sighed in relief.

Very slowly, a couple of footsteps at a time, I carried the pack box to her. I soothed the mare with her name and with my voice. I let her smell the box. She watched me out of the corner of her eye as I tied the heavy pack box on her left side, gabbing all the time.

Now she had to stand unbalanced while I got the other box. "Society Girl, good girl," I murmured. "Yeah, I bet it feels awful with all that weight hanging on just one side. Don't worry, we'll soon have you back in balance with this other box."

She never moved. With no problems at all, I tied the pack box on her right-hand side. I patted her. "You are a good girl. And you're smart too, aren't you, Society Girl. You do learn fast. Just like Mrs. Longhurst said."

Next the tarp had to go over the whole pack. That went amazingly well. She snorted a bit, but talking softly to her and saying her name worked like magic.

Time for the lash rope. I flipped the rope under her belly. Then I tied it around both boxes. Now to tighten everything. I rubbed her neck. "Society Girl. Are you ready? This is going to feel weird." I pulled slowly on the rope, chatting as it tightened all around her. She kept listening, standing quietly.

When I finished tying the knot, she turned her head from side to side to check the pack. Then she stood watching me as though to say, "Now what?"

Now I had to walk her around. This is when some horses erupt. I untied her. She took a couple of steps. She stopped when she heard the noise of the cans in her pack. I let her think it over. "Society Girl, that little bit of rattling is okay," I said gently. "It won't hurt you. Society Girl, good girl."

I led her forward another step, and then a few more. Within moments she had accepted her new duties, and we were ready to go.

I let Star loose. She would follow us

into camp all by herself. Down the trail I headed, riding Dusty and leading the new pack horse.

I turned to look at her. Society Girl was a good-looking horse. No one would ever guess how old she was. If they asked, I'd tell them the auctioneer didn't say. That was true. He didn't.

"Society Girl," I murmured. She lifted her head, her ears forward. "How could you like having such a dumb name?" I said, laughing.

I'd never figured out a nickname so people wouldn't have to use *my* dumb names. Amby? That's what you'd call a baby. Brose? Yuck! A nickname from Virgil? Forget it!

But I had to think of a good name for this horse. It looked like she might be a keeper after all, so she'd need a name. Each of her legs was white up to the knee, like long stockings. "Stocking?" No, that would be a dumb name too. I looked at her blaze, the wide white stripe running down the front of her face. "Blaze" could be her name.

"Blaze," I called. Of course she didn't respond, just kept plodding along.

The path became narrow as we rode through a thick spruce forest. Society Girl — no, Blaze — crashed one of her pack boxes against the trunk of a huge tree. The force threw her off balance. She almost fell. Terrified, she looked around. She was trying to understand what had happened.

Only once more did she hit one of her boxes against a tree. After that she had it figured out. When the trail passed too close to a tree, she'd swing her whole belly out of the way. It took most pack horses quite a while to learn to do that, and a few never did. Surely Uncle Mac couldn't help but accept such a smart horse.

Society Girl perked up her ears when we saw a deer across the river and then later a few elk in a meadow. Uncle Mac loved alert, intelligent horses. Maybe this would work out okay.

It still wasn't dark when we reached base camp. Summer evenings in Alberta's mountains stay light until after ten o'clock. It was only nine o'clock when I reached our camp, but I was exhausted. It had been quite a day. Up at five this morning. Two hours, ride each way. Three hours each way rattling over gravel roads in the truck. Shopping for camp groceries. Letting go of Blackie. Buying the new horse. I was worn out, weak from hunger, but didn't feel I'd be able to keep anything in my stomach.

I rode down the hill towards the horse corrals and huge canvas tents at the edge of the meadow. I sure hoped I wouldn't have to visit all night with the "dudes." That's what we called the trail-riding customers, but never to their faces.

The eleven dudes were sitting around the campfire, talking and laughing. They looked up at the new horse and me. Uncle Mac sauntered over, his eyes glued on Society Girl. Aunt Madge followed — and, of course, Janice too. She strolled behind, her head tilted in that scornful way. I already knew which one would give me a hard time.

Chapter Four

"What a pretty horse," Aunt Madge said.

Uncle Mac ran his hands over Society Girl's muscles. "Strong too," he added.

I pulled my face into a smile. I knew that none of them would say anything about Blackie, even though he was on everybody's mind. We'd all loved him, even Janice.

"How much did she cost?" Uncle Mac

asked, patting the new horse.

"Nine-twenty." I handed him what was left from the $200 he had sent. He counted the money and nodded.

"Did you talk to her owner before the sale?" Janice asked.

I shook my head. They'd believe me. Lots of people left their horses to sell at the auction and just picked up their money later.

Janice kept watching me out of the corner of her eye. "You don't know anything about this horse?"

"The auctioneer claimed she was trained for harness and riding." I spoke as calmly as possible. "He said little kids can ride her too. Probably never packed before — she was a bit afraid at first. But she took to it just fine."

Uncle Mac fingered the wrinkles above the horse's eyes. "The only thing that worries me," he said, "is that she looks a bit old. A few gray hairs too." He opened the horse's mouth. She gagged, but stood motionless while he stared in at her teeth. "Smooth mouth. Bet she's not just fifteen though."

"She's probably eighteen or maybe even more," Janice said. "Trust Ambrose to get a horse that's ready for a seniors' lodge."

I winced. "She's a strong horse," I said.

"Strength isn't everything." Uncle Mac spoke gently. "Mountains are awful hard on an old horse. Especially carrying a big, heavy, deadweight pack into high country. Their lungs and hearts have a hard time."

"Well," I said, "maybe at first she could carry kids. For a couple of weeks or so. If she didn't have too much weight to carry, she'd get used to the altitude faster."

Janice sighed and stuffed her hands into her pockets. "A horse this old might never build up enough lung power to carry a heavy pack over the top of a mountain."

"Maybe she could carry kids the rest of the summer," I said. "We could pack one of the kids' horses."

Janice snorted. "None of our kids' horses are built right for packing. We need a big, strong, young pack horse. We don't need another kids' horse. We've got lots of them.

Ambrose, you should be a social worker instead of a cowboy."

"Just forget it," I said. "This mare can pack. Right away. She'll do fine."

Uncle Mac looked at Janice. "Well," he said, "there's another horse sale coming up. If the mare doesn't work out, she can go to the auction again next Saturday. The meat buyers will . . . Well, we can't lose much."

He slapped his big hand against Society Girl's neck. "Who knows, old girl, you might be a good pack horse. Ambrose might even want you instead of his summer wages . . ." His voice faded off again. He was thinking of Blackie.

Aunt Madge put her hand on my shoulder, as though she was giving me a hug. "Did you find out the horse's name?" she asked softly.

I shook my head, feeling terrible. I hated to think of myself as a coward *and* a liar. But there was no way I could dare tell the truth about any of this.

"Well, she'll need a good name," said Aunt Madge. "Nice big animal like that." My aunt was smiling and I could tell she liked this new horse.

"I . . . uh . . . thought we could call her Blaze," I stammered.

"Blaze it is then," said Aunt Madge. Uncle Mac nodded.

The dudes had been listening. Now a few of them came over to pat the new horse.

"Ambrose, you better go eat," Aunt Madge said. "We can unpack these two horses. You go get some supper."

Janice was watching me. She never would have eaten before unpacking the horses.

But I needed to be alone, so I turned and headed to the huge canvas cook tent. A wisp of smoke was still coming out of the campstove chimney.

My supper was in the oven of the old woodstove — baked ham, scalloped potatoes, canned corn. There was even a huge piece of apple pie on the table, and fresh bread too. Aunt Madge baked wonderful things in the oven of that little woodstove.

I still didn't feel like eating anything. I dished up some food and sat down, leaning my elbows on the faded plastic tablecloth. It was getting dark, especially in the tent. But if I lit the gas lantern, some of the dudes would probably come wandering in for a visit.

Tomorrow was a big day. Janice and I had to move two of our customers — Mr. Friesen and his bratty ten-year-old son Ryan — to Wapta Lake. That meant five hours of hard riding over a steep mountain pass.

Mr. Friesen was a famous nature photographer. He wanted a week at Wapta Lake to take pictures for a wildflower book. Janice and I would have to pack everything the four of us would need for the whole week.

Plenty of people had heard about Wapta Lake's fantastic fishing and wildflowers, but because of the awful trail up there, few people ever went to Wapta. The trail would be quite a test for Society Girl.

I'd never been to Wapta either, and I felt worried about the trip. Things were very busy. We were all overworked, so Janice and

I had to do this on our own. At least Janice had been there a couple of times before.

It was getting too dark to see anything in the cook tent. I gave in, lit the lantern and hung it from the ridgepole. Then I grabbed an old newspaper to take my mind off things while I poked away at my supper. The hiss of the lamp and the warm yellow circle of light surrounded me in a world all my own.

I didn't even look up when the tent flap opened. But I could tell it was Ryan Friesen the minute he called, "Hi, Ambrose."

I mumbled hello and kept flipping through the newspaper. That kid was the last person I felt like talking to. Ever since he had arrived in camp, he'd been nothing but trouble.

He had taken our last jar of peanut butter and smeared it on a tree to feed the squirrels. He had poured a pail of ice-cold river water over the top of the hot cookstove because it "sizzled so neat." He'd put a loaf of Aunt Madge's fresh-baked bread into the creek just to see if it would float.

"Hey, Ambrose," Ryan called again.

I tried to ignore him and kept reading.

"Look here, Ambrose. I'm a cowboy," Ryan drawled.

I glanced up. That skinny little kid had my lariat, twirling it around his head. "Hey, give me that," I said.

He grinned and kept twirling the rope.

A person's lariat is something you don't fool around with. It has to be coiled exactly the same each time, otherwise it gets kinks in it and won't throw straight. "Gimme that rope," I said again.

"Why?"

"Because nobody touches my rope, that's why."

Ryan kept twirling the rope above his curly brown hair. I leaped up and tried to grab the lariat. "Give it to me!" I shouted. I didn't have much talent handling little brats.

The flap of the cook tent opened again. Mr. Friesen strode in. Without a word he grabbed the rope from Ryan, handed it to me and pulled the kid out of the tent.

A couple of minutes later, Mr. Friesen was back. I sighed and put down my paper.

"Sorry about that," he said. "The kid's been allowed to run wild too long. I keep telling my ex-wife — it's better that Ryan cries now than we cry later. She doesn't see it. She's always babied him too much. It doesn't help that they're living with his grandma and grandpa. Grandparents let a kid get away with everything."

I nodded. As if I knew anything about all of that.

He finally took a breath. "Ryan needs something there on his grandparents' farm to teach him respect and responsibility. I thought a horse might be good for him. But every horse I get for him just ends up bucking him off or running away."

No wonder, I thought. I hated seeing Ryan dig his heels into the cute little horse named Velvet we'd chosen for him to ride to Spruce Falls the day before.

Ryan felt he was quite a cowboy, kicking Velvet in the ribs and yanking her reins.

He even tried to make her gallop through deep mud when it was pouring rain. That was the first time I'd ever seen Velvet refuse to obey.

No, Ryan sure wouldn't bring out the best in a horse, I thought to myself. But all I said was, "A good kids' horse is hard to find."

"Yeah," Mr. Friesen said, "all the ones for sale seem to be stubborn ponies or spoiled horses."

I thought of how great Society Girl would be for kids. But never for a brat like Ryan Friesen, that was for sure.

Chapter Five

Every well-used camp in the Rocky Mountains has a kind of bird called the whiskey-jack. Whiskey-jacks get very tame around people. In fact, they learn to steal food. Uncle Mac's base camp had some of the boldest whiskey-jacks anywhere.

The next morning, when the dudes were eating around the campfire, a whiskey-jack flew down. The bird perched on the edge of a guy's plate. Before the surprised man could yell, the whiskey-jack grabbed a whole pancake and carried it off into a tree.

Ryan Friesen got the idea he'd catch that bird. He took one of our empty wooden pack boxes as a trap. He propped one end of the box upside down on a stick. He tied a string to the stick so he could easily yank the stick out. For bait Ryan set pieces of pancake on the ground inside the propped-up box.

Janice and I were folding a big canvas tent to take along to Wapta. I looked over at Ryan. He was lying on his stomach with the end of the string in his hand. He was waiting for the bird to try to steal the pancake.

I should have been glad to have something crazy like that to take my mind off Blackie, but instead I just felt more upset. "The stupid kid never even asked if he could use that pack box," I mumbled to Janice.

"You don't have time to worry about a dumb kid trying to trap a whiskey-jack," she said. "We've got enough to worry about just getting the Friesens packed up to Wapta."

I grabbed a pack box and began jamming in groceries. Janice said, "Ambrose, don't forget to wrap newspaper around the butter and cheese and frozen meat. Otherwise they'll all be boiling by the time we get there."

Biting my lip, I nodded. Of course I would not have forgotten. With hardly a cloud in the sky, anybody could tell it was going to be a hot day. I didn't need her bossing me around, telling me how to do my job.

Janice was getting the pack horses ready. Mr. Friesen came over, dragging a heavy tripod. Then he brought over three huge cameras, about ten lenses, and a stack of almost a dozen thick botany books.

"You can't take all that stuff," Janice said. "Mac has to pack the other nine trail riders to Blue Lake for a few days, so we're short of pack horses this week."

"I need everything," Mr. Friesen said.

Janice rolled her eyes. "Why would

anybody need three monstrous cameras?"

Mr. Friesen's voice rose. "I use a different speed of film in each camera. I'm paying you good money to take all of this up there."

Janice put her hands on her hips. "I don't care how much money you're paying. We still get only three pack horses this week. Three pack horses for the four of us. We need room for two tents, four sleeping bags, some horse feed, and groceries for us all week. Or were you planning to eat your textbooks and your cameras?"

When the shouting started, Uncle Mac had to step in. Finally Mr. Friesen agreed to take just two cameras, a few of the lenses, three books and, of course, his tripod. But he wasn't too happy.

During all of this, Ryan was lying on his belly trying to trap a whiskey-jack. Every time he pulled the string, the bird would fly out just before the box crashed to the ground. And usually the bird would get a piece of pancake too.

I guess Mr. Friesen had to take his anger out on somebody. He went striding over to Ryan and told him to quit being so foolish. He made the kid get up off the ground and said what a pig he was. That was true enough, what with dirt and grass stains all over the front of the kid's T-shirt.

But that put Ryan in a bad mood. He stomped over to where I was tightening the little saddle on Velvet. He asked me why he had to ride that dumb, boring horse again.

I got really mad and told Ryan he could ride one of the whiskey-jacks for all I cared. He said he might just do that.

When we were packing Society Girl, I could sure see trouble coming. "These horses are still loaded way too heavy," I told Janice. "We'll each have to leave something behind. Just for this time couldn't you do without your big pillow or a couple of your thick western novels?"

"Are you saying your new pack horse is too elderly or too feeble to carry anything?" Janice's eyes narrowed. "Then maybe you should pack your riding horse. If not, just pile everything on that poor old mare and keep quiet."

It wasn't easy to stand up to Janice, but by this time I was so mad I didn't care. "Since when did you become the boss of this outfit?" I asked.

That upset Uncle Mac. He said Janice had worked hard all these years and no one had the right to insult her.

By the time we had the horses ready, we were all in a rotten mood, all except Aunt Madge. And that was just because no one had happened to find anything to yell at her about.

When we headed off, Ryan wrenched Velvet's head around. Then he rammed his heels against the little horse's ribs.

Janice stopped her horse, glaring at Ryan with a look that would have scalded milk. "Now listen here, kid," she said. "If you do that one more time, you'll walk — all the way. You treat Velvet with respect. Or else. Have you got that?"

Ryan just nodded. I guess he realized he'd better not say one word. No one else dared speak either.

We headed up the trail. The three pack horses swayed from the weight they were carrying. I hated to see them loaded that heavy. I kept telling myself it was just for five hours. They'd have a week's rest while we camped. And they'd have much less to carry on the way home. A lot of the weight was groceries and horse feed, which we'd be using in the days ahead.

It's hard for anybody to stay mad when riding through mountain forests. The cooler air was sweet with the smell of spruce. In between the trees, thick green moss made furry wall-to-wall carpeting. Everything was so beautiful. And the trail didn't seem too difficult. I sighed and started to feel much better.

But within an hour the trail became bad and then worse, steeper by the minute. Obviously not many people used this trail. The poor horses had to lift their legs high over rotted trees that lay like hurdles across the path.

We rode quite a while along a narrow sandy ledge high above the river. Clumps of sand fell down into the water as we passed. Straight down. If a horse missed one footstep, that horse and its cargo would be far below in the river.

Uncle Mac never would have sent Janice and me on a trail like this if things weren't so busy. In fact, he and Aunt Madge — just the two of them — had to pack and cook for nine dudes while we looked after only two this week. The outfitting business was a hard life. I could have made more money at any other summer job. Still, being in the mountains and working around horses made up for it all.

Back in the forest, the path became even steeper. We came to a rock slide that had tumbled down ages ago, all along the side of a mountain. The horses scraped between boulders as big as cars, swinging their packs out of the way. They climbed higher, struggling for footing on shiny solid rock.

All the horses were soaked with sweat and gasping for air. We stopped often to let them rest. But it was taking too long for Society Girl to catch her breath. Her head hung low and her legs were starting to wobble as she crawled up the steeper places. What if I'd rescued her at the auction only to see her die in the mountains?

Chapter Six

I was used to steep rocky trails, but this was ridiculous. The trail — if you could call it a trail — twisted upward between jagged rocks. It was as narrow as a curved playground slide.

Sweat ran, white and foamy, down the horses' shoulders and legs like soapsuds. What hot, humid weather! I found myself wishing for the thunderstorm that usually came with such a hot day. At least it would cool things off.

We reached a bank that looked impossible — almost straight up and so rocky. All of the horses would need a rest before they tackled that bank. "This is the worst part of the trail," Janice said. "Then it soon gets a lot better."

Society Girl couldn't seem to quit gasping. "See, she looks strong," Janice said, "but the poor old thing just doesn't have the lungs for climbing mountains."

"How much longer?" Ryan called to us. "When are we ever going to get there?"

Janice answered. "We're only about an hour from the lake."

I looked at my watch. Five o'clock already.

Janice's horse headed up the bank, his legs bent as though he were crawling. I shouted, "Janice, isn't there some other way around this?"

She stopped to let her riding horse and pack horse catch their breath again. "Yeah," she hollered back. "If you have a helicopter." Janice seemed worried as she turned to look at me. "You think your old gal can make it?"

I pulled Society Girl's halter rope as we headed upward. Within seconds my poor mare sounded like a steam engine. And she was loaded way too heavy for her age. Janice was right. Society Girl was too old for this. I wasn't being fair to her.

The horses' iron shoes scraped, metal against solid stone. Slowly they struggled upward, legs bent, lungs wheezing. Society Girl's halter rope tightened in my hand. I looked back. The old mare was really having problems. Groaning, she put her head down and lurched over one of the big rocks, her shoes slipping.

Then, as though in slow motion, she crumpled to the ground. There she lay on her side, her rump jammed against a boulder. One back leg was twisted up under her belly. Blood ran from a scrape above one hoof.

I jumped off Dusty and bent over Society Girl, yanking at her head. "Get up," I yelled in panic. My hands were shaking.

The old horse groaned, looking at me, her eyes glazed. Then her head stretched out to lie limp against a rock, her eyelids closed. She moaned. Her lips parted, showing her teeth and tongue. It looked like she was having a heart attack.

"You have to get up." I was pleading, trying to revive her, trying to get through to her. Her long straight eyelashes lay closed, dark brown against her face.

Frantically I glanced around. Ryan and his dad were off their horses too. They stood at the base of the bank, looking up at us, frightened.

Janice left her horses and slid down the bank. She began pushing against the old mare's rump. I pushed too, my muscles straining, but found it hard to get footing on such a steep incline.

Society Girl's breathing wasn't heavy anymore. In fact, it was shallow. Too shallow. She was fading out on us.

"Get up," I yelled, my voice much too

shrill. "Please get up. Don't die. Come on, please get up." Hooking my hands in her halter, I lifted her heavy head and pulled with all my strength. But when I let go, her head flopped back down on the rock.

The mare wasn't moving at all now. A fine mess I'd got this animal into. Yeah, I'd been the big hero to rescue her from the meat buyers. Rescue her! She'd have been better off dying in a slaughterhouse than out here like this.

Poor Mrs. Longhurst would be in her one tiny room in Edmonton, wondering how her horse was doing. Good thing she couldn't see Society Girl now.

"Ambrose, don't just stand there," Janice yelled. "We have to get her pack off. Loosen her cinches!"

What good would it do? The horse was dying. Right here in front of us.

Janice crawled over the huge boulder, pushing me aside. She untied the knot and yanked the rope off. Society Girl's pack came loose. A sleeping bag rolled down the hill, bouncing. Mr. Friesen scrambled to catch it.

I grabbed the pack box and flung it aside as Janice loosened both cinches.

Still the mare lay motionless, hardly breathing. Janice slapped at the horse's face and neck, grabbed one of her hooves and shook it, trying to get some response. Somehow we had to get through to her. We had to get this horse to fight to keep living.

Kneeling beside Janice, I rubbed the mare's face and called, "Society Girl. Come on, Society Girl, get up."

"*Society Girl*?" asked Janice, lifting her eyebrows. "That's her name?"

"Yeah," I said and kept calling to the horse, rubbing her face. The mare's eyelashes flickered.

Then Janice called, "Society Girl. Come on, Society Girl. You have to get up. Society Girl." The horse's big head moved against the rock. Together we called again, "Society Girl." One eye opened. She groaned, her lips moving.

Janice jumped up. She scrambled up the bank, grabbed her canteen from the saddle and headed back down. She splashed water over Society Girl's open mouth.

The horse's tongue licked out at the water. We both cheered as though we were winning a football game. Janice poured the water from the canteen more carefully now. She poured it just a little at a time, directly onto Society Girl's tongue. The mare kept licking for more water. We kept calling, rubbing her face, pushing at her shoulder. Society Girl groaned again and lifted her head. Both eyes opened. Her feet began moving.

Then the horse took a deep breath. "Get out of the way," Janice yelled. "She's going to try to get up!"

Society Girl's free back leg kicked out a couple of times. She shook her whole body and lay for a moment gasping. Then with a powerful lurch, that horse pushed her front legs straight out, trying to pry herself up.

We put all our weight against her, pushing from the side and from behind. She lurched again, moaning, scrambling against the rocks.

And then she was standing. She was trembling, her head bent — but she was standing. And I knew I'd never ask Society Girl to carry that pack again. No matter what.

Chapter Seven

Ryan and his dad had left their horses and crawled up the bank. Together we stood watching Society Girl. She shook herself and looked around.

Blood still ran down her leg, but it was starting to clot. The other scrapes didn't look too bad at all.

We let her stand resting for a few min-

horses down too much. It seemed as though he read my mind. "I'm sorry," he mumbled, so quietly I wasn't even sure he'd spoken.

"We can pack Dusty instead," I said. Then I pointed to the old mare. "I'll walk and lead her. My saddle isn't heavy. It can go on Society Girl . . . uh . . . Blaze . . . "

They all laughed. "Society Girl — that's quite a name," said Janice. "Where did you get it from?"

"Uh . . . they said it was her name. But I changed it. Thought it didn't sound like a normal name for a horse."

"You got that right," said Janice.

Ryan snickered. "It's just about as crazy as your name, Ambrose."

To my surprise, Janice glared at Ryan. Then she patted the mare on the shoulder. "Yeah, Society Girl," said Janice, looking sad. "You're a brave old thing to get back up again, aren't you?"

I couldn't believe my ears. Janice almost sounded like someone with a heart.

utes. Then Janice said, "Well, let's see if we can get her out of here."

I pulled on Society Girl's halter rope. She shuffled forward, limping on her cut leg. Then up over the boulder she lurched to a more level place.

Every time I pulled her rope, she moved a bit farther. She climbed, favoring the cut leg. After a few more steps she was hardly limping at all. We were almost to the top of the terrible incline. Janice had said the trail would get easier after this bank. Society Girl was still puffing, but she could probably make it to Wapta as long as she had no weight to carry.

We let her rest again. "Now what?" Janice asked. Scattered below us were all the things that had been on Society Girl.

"She can't carry that pack anymore," I said, half-expecting Janice to snap at me.

Janice didn't say a word, just nodded.

I looked down at all the stuff on the ground, then at Mr. Friesen, feeling angry. It was mostly his junk that had weighed the

We soon had Dusty loaded sky-high and headed off again, with Janice and her pack horse at the front of the line. I walked at the end, leading Society Girl, my empty stirrups swinging.

It was true, this part of the trail was not quite as steep. And Society Girl was walking well for what she'd been through. Still, she could go only about half as fast as normal. Over and over again, everybody had to stop to wait for us. Finally I said, "You guys go ahead."

Mr. Friesen seemed to be feeling bad about the whole business. "I'll help unpack and set up the tents," he said.

I nodded. "You guys might even get supper started before I get there."

Janice frowned. "I don't like the idea of you being on this trail by yourself, Ambrose. What if that horse can't make it? You'd have to leave her alone to get help. Anyway, we're only about half an hour from camp now."

"That means it's probably going to take

Society Girl an hour. You go ahead. I'll be all right on my own. She's going to make it."

"Ryan could stay back with you," said Mr. Friesen. "If anything went wrong, he could run ahead to let us know."

Janice was the one who answered. "Sure." She smirked. "Why not?"

"I'll be fine on my own," I said, scowling at her.

"No, it's a good idea," Janice said. "Ryan can walk, leading Velvet behind Society Girl."

Ryan was grinning like crazy. This was a big adventure for him. So I guess it was all decided.

When they started off, Janice called over her shoulder, "Bye, Ambrose. Have fun."

I gritted my teeth and made a face at her, but she'd already turned her horses to head up the trail.

Then Ryan and I were on our own. I walked slowly, trying not to listen to Society Girl's rasping breath as she scrambled over rocks and fallen trees. Ryan followed, leading Velvet.

At first the trail was too rough for much talking, but gradually Ryan put his motor-mouth in gear. It was almost a relief to have Ryan there to be annoyed at. It took my mind off my real problem. What was I going to do with Society Girl? I was scared to realize how much I already cared about her.

When we stopped to rest, I stroked the mare's sweaty neck. She touched her soft nose against my face.

Ryan broke into my thoughts. "So now she has to go for meat, huh?" he said. "No-body will want a horse that falls down all the time."

"She doesn't fall down all the time," I said. "Just once. And it's your dad's junk that loaded the pack horses too heavy."

"See how much she's puffing now," said Ryan.

"So are you." I was trying not to shout. "Anybody puffs climbing mountains when they aren't used to it."

Ryan shook his head. "I heard what your uncle said last night. She'll bring lots of money for meat. Then you guys can buy a good horse."

"She is a good horse! It's just that mountains are hard on her because she's kind of old. Society Girl would do just fine for ordinary riding or harness work."

"How do they kill 'em?" asked Ryan. "Do they shoot them, or what?"

I didn't dare look at him because if he said one more word, I'd strangle that kid.

Chapter Eight

Even when the trail eased, Society Girl was still breathing too hard.

We reached the windy mountain pass. Blue snow-ridged mountains surrounded us. Ryan hardly noticed the view. "Is Janice your girlfriend?" he asked.

I groaned and gave him a dirty look. What had I done to deserve this kid?

"I've got a sister at home," said Ryan. "She's your age. Maybe she could be your girlfriend."

We went down the other side of the mountain, our horses' hooves scraping on the rocks. The path became quite easy past some runty spruce trees. Society Girl was breathing normally again. She began walking a bit faster too, but still seemed very tired.

Finally we rounded a corner and saw a small turquoise lake far below us. Beside it was our canvas tent and Janice's little nylon tent. Wildflowers grew all around, an unbelievable carpet of colors.

As we headed down the mountain, we smelled steak cooking over the campfire. "Do we have to eat steak again?" asked Ryan. "When are we going to roast some hot dogs?"

I gave him another dirty look.

We were soon settled at camp, eating supper. All of us seemed too tired and hungry to talk, even Ryan.

After doing dishes, Janice and I led the horses to the lake for water, then tied them to the trees for the night. "I bet you enjoyed that last hour on the trail — just you and Ryan together," she said, grinning. I made a face. We both laughed. Neither of us said anything about Society Girl.

When we got back to camp we found Ryan sound asleep, curled in a tarp beside the pack boxes in the big canvas tent. I held the flashlight while Mr. Friesen unrolled their sleeping bags. He lifted his son and zippered him under the covers without waking him. I put my bedroll beside theirs and settled in for the night too.

I could hear Janice moving around quite a while before she put out the campfire and went to sleep in her tent.

The next morning Society Girl seemed pretty stiff. But after I led her around a few minutes, she moved more easily. The cut on her leg and the other scrapes didn't look too bad. I began to feel a little better.

Everybody else seemed to be in a good mood as we ate breakfast. But that meant

Ryan was blabbing so much I wished Uncle Mac had supplied us with earplugs.

While Janice and I did dishes, Mr. Friesen headed up into the meadows. He had to make a couple of trips for all his books, cameras and his tripod. "Those flowers are incredible," he said. His eyes were shining as he headed back to the meadow.

Janice handed Ryan a dish towel. He dried a couple of plates, got tired of that, threw the dish towel on an old log and walked off.

"Hey, watch where you put things!" Janice said, shaking the towel out. "Look, it's all dirty. Why do you think we pound nails into the poor old trees? It's for hanging things up so they keep clean and dry."

Ryan mumbled that this was worse than being around his dad.

After lunch Janice and I had to get firewood for cooking meals. In mountain camps, people always leave some firewood stacked for the next campers, but we had used most of that since we'd arrived. Now we had to search the nearby forest for a couple of dead trees that were still standing. We had to saw the trees down by hand. Then we'd ride back to camp, our horses each dragging a tree tied to a lariat wrapped around the saddle horn.

Ryan begged to come along. "No way," Janice said. "You'd probably stand under a tree when we're cutting it down."

I picked up my saddle and headed towards Dusty, then changed my mind. I'd ride Society Girl. Janice would see this was a good horse.

When I set the saddle on Society Girl, Janice scowled. "You're determined to kill that animal," she said.

"It's much cooler today," I said. "It will be a short ride. And I'm not nearly as heavy as the pack she carried yesterday. Who knows, for the rest of the summer I might ride her and pack Dusty."

Janice didn't answer. We rode over a steep forested slope looking for trees suitable for firewood. If a tree has fallen and partly rotted, its wood doesn't burn easily and doesn't give much heat for cooking either. It just makes thick, black, acidic smoke that stings your eyes. If you cut a living tree for firewood, it burns even worse. So we had to find dead, solid, standing trees.

Partway up the second steep bank we spotted a few dead trees standing at the top of the slope. Society Girl was gasping again. We stopped so she could catch her breath. "See, it wasn't just the pack or the hot day," Janice declared. "*You're* even too heavy for that horse when she's climbing mountains."

"She's still not all rested up from yesterday," I said. "And it'll take her a while to get in condition. She's just not used to the altitude."

Janice sneered. "Ambrose Metford, do you want to know something? It tears my guts out to see that poor old horse so tired, doing her best, just killing herself trying . . ." Janice hung her head. "It makes me think of my mom."

I shifted in the saddle, my mouth gaping. "Your mom?"

"Yeah, my mom. And don't bother to act so shocked. Do you know how awful it feels to be a little kid watching your mom go out every day to scrub floors? She had to work like a dog to feed us kids and our drunken dad. She'd come home to us so tired, with hours more work at home."

"I . . . uh . . . Janice, I'm sorry."

"I don't want your pity. We don't need anybody's pity." Her voice was deadly. "I just want you to know it's not right to keep pushing that horse. It's not right to abuse anything or anybody just because they have the spirit to keep going."

I didn't know how to answer, and she didn't say anything more.

Without talking we cut down a couple of dead trees and dragged them back to camp. I dragged the smaller one with Society Girl.

Chapter Nine

The next day was hot again and we did have an afternoon thunderstorm. Mr. Friesen came running from the meadow, loaded with cameras, books and notes. He raced to get everything in the canvas tent, safe from the heavy rain.

We all sat in the big tent, listening to the thunder crashing. "What about the horses?" Ryan asked. "Aren't they scared?"

"We have so many thunderstorms in the mountains," Janice said. "These horses are used to thunder and lightning. They hardly act jumpy at all in a storm."

"Mountain weather is crazy," I added, turning to Mr. Friesen. "It can be hot and clear one moment, then thundering and raining — maybe even snowing — the next. We always have to take along heavy jackets and rain slickers when we ride."

"At least it hardly ever hails in the mountains," said Janice. "Rain, wind, lightning — and snow — they're bad enough. Hail forms high up, but it usually falls lower down, in the foothills or on the prairies."

We sat talking as rain poured on the tent. After a while, Ryan began complaining about how boring it was to do nothing for a whole week.

So I just had to put my big foot in my mouth. Uncle Mac had talked about some fossils in huge boulders farther along the trail. I told Ryan maybe we could all go for a ride one day to see the fossils.

"Fossils?" asked Ryan, his eyes wide. "What kind of fossils?"

"Uncle Mac says there's thousands of fossils of seashells and leaves and everything," I said, excited too. "He's even seen a fossil of part of a fish there. Uncle Mac told me the boulders are full of fossils. We just keep following the trail we came in on. The place should be easy to find."

"Seashells! And a fish fossil? Way up here in the mountains?" Ryan's mouth gaped open. "Let's go this afternoon. As soon as it quits raining. Please."

I realized then that Janice was glaring at me. Why had I even mentioned fossils?

Ryan would not let the subject drop. From that moment on there was no peace. He wanted to see the fossils, and the sooner the better.

"I could ride there by myself if you're all too busy," said Ryan the next morning as we ate our breakfast. "Ambrose said it would be easy to find. And there's just one trail. I could saddle Velvet and go by my-self."

"Don't you dare," Mr. Friesen said.

Janice chuckled. "Not much to worry about there. A kid could never get Velvet to leave on her own no matter how he tried. She's used to having other horses with her every-where."

I nodded. "*We'd* even have a hard time getting one of these horses to go up the trail alone, away from camp," I said. "As soon as horses have been together a week or so, they don't want to leave each other. It's just a horse's nature."

"Dad, I could help you get done taking pictures. Then we could all ride to the fos-sils."

"We'll see," his father said.

Ryan did try hard to help his dad that morning, moving the tripod, carrying books, holding camera lenses, but he was becoming more and more restless. Mr. Friesen got more and more involved with his work, paying even less attention to Ryan.

Maybe it wasn't so smart to leave the two of them alone, but that afternoon Janice and I had to get firewood again. This time I was riding Dusty so Society Girl could rest up.

"When you guys get back, could we go see the fossils?" Ryan asked. "I could have Velvet saddled, all ready to ride."

"When we get back we have to saw the firewood and make supper," Janice said.

After we rode up the mountainside and cut a couple of dead trees, we both sat staring over the valley. The only noise was the drone of insects in the wildflowers around us.

It felt good to get away from camp and do absolutely nothing for a few minutes, especially on such a hot, humid afternoon. But I wished I could keep my churning mind from thinking about either Blackie or Society Girl.

Janice broke the silence. "Ambrose, you talked to Society Girl's former owner, didn't you?"

Shocked, I tried to meet her eyes. "What makes you think that?"

"Because no auctioneer on this earth

would ever tell people that a horse was named Society Girl. So you must have met her owner."

I pulled a piece of grass. "What if I did?"

"I think you know how old that horse really is."

I took a deep breath. "Would you believe twenty-five?"

"Yes, I would." The tone of her voice was strange, almost soft. Then I found myself telling her the whole story. She listened. She didn't even interrupt or make fun of me. Why had I bothered to lie?

"Now if only I could think of a smart way out of this," I said.

"The smart thing," said Janice, "would have been not to buy such an old horse in the first place."

"I'm sorry I told you."

"Calm down," she said. "I'm on your side."

I leaned my face against my knees. "If I could just hold onto Society Girl until we're done for the summer," I said. "Then I'd have time to find her a good home. Put some ads in the paper."

Janice sighed. "Ambrose, we need another pack horse now. Uncle Mac doesn't have the money to buy one, and you sure don't either. You'll have to sell Society Girl. This week."

I shook my head. "She'd make such a good riding horse for the kids out here."

"You managed somehow to let go of Blackie," Janice said. "How come you're being so stubborn about Society Girl?"

"Because she's alive and well. And because of Blackie too. You just wouldn't understand."

"All I know," Janice said, "is that it never pays to be a bleeding heart."

"Well at least I have a heart!" I snapped at her.

Janice laughed. "Some people have to be heartless to survive. Maybe it gets to be a habit."

We climbed on our horses and headed

back towards camp. Each of us was dragging a big tree with our lariats. "Too bad Ryan is such a rotten kid," Janice said a few minutes later. "Otherwise you could sell Society Girl to him."

"Ryan?" I shuddered. "I wouldn't wish that kid on a grizzly bear! No, maybe there'll be somebody as dumb as me at the auction next week."

"I think you'd have better odds with Ryan." Janice was trying to keep smiling, but she looked worried too.

"Hey," Janice said as we rode into camp, "where is Society Girl?"

All the other horses were still there, tied to trees. A stump of wood had been rolled in, right beside where Society Girl had been tied. The stump was high enough for a kid to stand on for saddling a very tall horse.

We galloped to the meadow. Mr. Friesen looked up as we pulled our horses to a stop.

"Where's Ryan?" Janice asked.

Mr. Friesen shrugged his shoulders. "I don't know. He's around somewhere."

"Oh, yeah?" said Janice. "Well, Society Girl's missing and so is your son. It doesn't take much of a detective to figure out where he's gone."

Mr. Friesen's face turned pale. "The fossils!" he said. "Oh, no! I'm coming with you."

For once Janice didn't argue. We rushed back to camp and flung a saddle on another horse. "When did you last see Ryan?" asked Janice.

Mr. Friesen shook his head. "I guess it would be at least an hour ago. Maybe two."

"Remember to tie your rain slicker on," said Janice. "With such a hot afternoon we'll probably get a thunderstorm. Bring Ryan's slicker along too."

Mr. Friesen searched the tent and around the camp. "Can't find it," he said. "Ryan must have taken his slicker with him."

"Hard to believe he did something right," mumbled Janice.

The three of us headed up the trail together at a fast trot. But the trail soon became too steep for trotting.

Gasping, the horses climbed. The heat wasn't making things any better. This would be hard on Society Girl. The trouble was, such a willing horse would never quit — not until it was too late.

Chapter Ten

When we stopped the horses for a rest, Mr. Friesen voiced my fear. "What if that old horse collapses? Like she did when we were packing in. Ryan could be lying pinned underneath her. Or she could have crumpled and slid with him down a cliff."

"Ryan hardly weighs anything," I said. "Society Girl collapsed only because she was loaded too heavy." My voice didn't sound convincing.

We had to stop often to let the horses catch their breath. The air felt so humid now, thick and muggy as a steam bath. The horses' coats were drenched with sweat.

I was getting scared. We climbed higher, along the side of a steep drop-off. I looked down, half expecting to see two bodies — a big red horse and a little boy.

The others were looking down too. We kept scanning the bottom of the ravine. But there was no one and nothing below, just moss, trees and rocks.

Finally the trail leveled. As we rode along we all stared into the forest, searching for any sign of them. Surely our young horses should have caught up to Society Girl by now, even with an hour's head start.

We passed through meadows full of wildflowers. Mr. Friesen didn't seem to notice the flowers. His face was tight and tired-looking as he gazed from side to side.

A wind had come up, strangely cool and

refreshing. Our horses must be glad of the wind. It would be easier on Society Girl too.

We started to climb again. There were fewer trees in this area, but we couldn't see far because of big shale ridges. The wind was blowing more strongly. The horses seemed unusually nervous.

"We're sure going to get our rainstorm," said Janice, holding her cowboy hat on. A huge cloud rolled over the crest of the mountain, rumbling, growing thick and dark. "Good thing Ryan has his raincoat along," she added. "There's not much shelter around here."

Soon we were riding through a high, open area. There was almost no shelter now, just some short scruffy trees, and once in a while a few big spruce far off the trail.

The temperature was dropping rapidly. Thunder growled over the mountain. Our horses were prancing. *That's strange*, I thought. Thunderstorms were part of their everyday life.

"I don't like it," Janice said. She pointed to the gigantic churning cloud moving down towards us. It had changed color, from blue-black to a creepy yellow-gray.

At first it was just rain, pouring suddenly, soaking us before we even got our rain slickers on. Then the wind swirled furiously. To my surprise, pellets of ice started falling, just a few at first, about the size of peas.

My horse, Dusty, arched his neck and snorted, curious. The other horses stopped and sniffed. They weren't used to hail. As I looked around, a tiny ice pellet bounced off my nose. I laughed nervously.

Within minutes no one was laughing. The hail was falling faster. Then bigger hailstones, like marbles, came crashing down on us. It hurt. The horses pulled hard against their reins, desperate to run.

"Head for those trees," Janice yelled, pointing to a few spruce far back on the trail. "Don't let the horses gallop or you'll never get them stopped." The wind and the roar of the hail muffled her words.

With all our strength, we held our horses in. I struggled to control Dusty as he leaped through the icy slush. Hailstones the size of golf balls were smashing down now. They beat my shoulders, even hammered my head through my thick cowboy hat.

The horses winced and snorted as hail battered them. Bruised from the hammering, they flung their heads around in panic.

The hail made so much noise that I couldn't even hear what Janice was shouting. My arms ached from pulling Dusty's reins. We were still so far from the trees. It was awful, the pain on my head, arms and shoulders increasing every second. I felt dizzy from pain. *We're being stoned to death*, I thought.

I had heard stories of animals and people killed by hailstones this big. First the hail knocks you unconscious . . .

Our horses weren't thinking. The pain was making them crazy. All they wanted was to run.

I reached the trees first. Somehow my arms found enough strength to pull Dusty to a stop.

Getting under the spruce trees gave instant relief from the beating of the hailstones. I jumped off Dusty.

Mr. Friesen's horse went thundering by. He couldn't stop it. Janice headed after them, her horse racing through the sloppy ice and mud.

Bending low over her animal's neck, Janice grabbed one of Mr. Friesen's reins. His horse spun around, then, flinching from the hailstones, reared up.

Terrified, Janice's horse reared too. Normally nothing could have made Janice fall from a horse, but she was already way off balance. Down she went.

I ran through the slamming hail towards Janice. She was lying in the slush. Her face and yellow raincoat were black with mud.

Mr. Friesen slid off his horse, still holding one of the reins. His horse reared again, trembling. It almost dragged him, but he yanked the animal in a circle to gain control.

I grabbed Janice's reins from her hands. Then Mr. Friesen and I pulled Janice and the two horses under the trees. All of us crowded in where Dusty was cowering.

The spruce trees were tall and narrow so the horses couldn't fit completely under the branches. We kept their heads right in by the tree trunks where hardly a hailstone got through the thick boughs. The animals stood trembling, cringing as hailstones crashed against their rumps.

All around us, hailstones pelted down, bouncing high, clattering. We stood beside the tree trunks, shivering, silent. I knew all three of us were wondering how Ryan could survive this.

The hail pounded and roared a few more minutes. The ground was covered in white. Then, like a tap turned off, the hail suddenly stopped. There was complete silence, a hush as though there could be no sound in all the world.

The air smelled icy fresh as the dark cloud moved on. Instantly, bright sunshine turned everything to gold. Even the thick blanket of hailstones covering the ground shone, golden.

We led our horses through the deep, crunchy hailstones back to the trail. What was once a dirt path had become a river. Slush, hailstones and mud ran swiftly downhill.

None of us had spoken yet. My head, shoulders and back throbbed from the beating they'd taken. I still felt dizzy.

Our horses had calmed down, but I knew they must be very sore. We had to climb on them anyway and splash up the muddy trail. We had to keep searching for Ryan, sick in our hearts, afraid of what we might find.

Chapter Eleven

We almost missed him. It was eagle-eyed Janice who spotted him far off the trail, by the edge of a ravine. A few big spruce trees sheltered a red-brown horse and a boy in a yellow raincoat.

We raced across the clearing to where Ryan sat on Society Girl. Bent over the saddle horn, shivering, he hugged the horse's soaking-wet neck.

He looked up at us as though he could hardly believe what he was seeing.

"Ryan!" his dad called, skidding his horse to a stop. Mr. Friesen jumped down, grabbing Ryan off the mare. "You're okay!"

"I sure was scared," Ryan said.

"How did you get over here?" his dad asked, hands trembling. "How did you get under these trees? You're so far from the path."

"She brought me here. I didn't know what to do. But Society Girl did. As soon as the hail started, she headed for these trees. She held her head down really low all the way. And we both just had to take it when it hurt so bad."

His dad was hugging him. "It was like being in a war," Ryan said, "like trillions of bullets hitting us. Like rocks dumped down from the sky. But Society Girl just kept on walking real calm, all the way to this tree."

Janice stroked Society Girl. "Sensible, aren't you? Maybe sometimes old is best. Not like these silly young horses that can't take some pain now and then."

Ryan tugged at his father's sleeve. "Dad, I gotta have this horse. She's my friend."

Mr. Friesen nodded, holding his son tighter.

Janice was watching me. She must have been waiting to see how I'd wiggle out of this without insulting Ryan too much.

I couldn't say anything, though, because I wasn't sure anymore what I wanted.

It seemed as though Janice thought she'd better help me say no to the Friesens. "Well," she said, "I don't think your son would be the best owner for this horse . . . "

She glanced at me, and I could hardly believe what she said next. "Anyhow, I think Ambrose was right all along. And when Mac hears what Society Girl did in the hailstorm, he'll agree. She should stay out here for kids to ride."

"But . . ." I sputtered.

"Yeah, we could pack one of the strongest of the kids' horses," she said, turning to me. "Just until there's money to buy a new pack horse. It's always scary when kids who have never ridden come out here in the mountains. We always worry that something awful might happen and some kid might get badly hurt. This sensible old horse would make it safer for us all."

What a crazy mixed-up thing. Here I was finally getting what I'd hoped for so badly — and now I wasn't sure.

I thought of Mrs. Longhurst. Would she want Society Girl on a farm with one rotten kid? Or would she want her horse in the mountains, carrying lots of children who would adore her?

Society Girl would harden up. She'd do well out here, and I'd get to be around her all the time to make sure she was treated well. It all made sense.

But then I stared at Ryan. He had his head pressed against Society Girl's face just the way Mrs. Longhurst had done. And his eyes looked so sad, just as hers had.

So this was one more time I'd have to trust my own feelings. "We'll miss her," I said, fighting to keep my voice normal. Ryan's eyes bugged out as he caught on. Pure joy spread across his face.

Janice wasn't smiling. "Ambrose, have you lost it?" she said. "Here I finally agree with you. And now you change your mind! Remember what you said about the grizzly bear?"

Ryan leaned his head back against the horse, troubled.

"Ambrose," said Janice, "you can take care of Society Girl out here. All the kids will love her. We'll have a horse we can trust totally — even with the most frightened beginners."

I shook my head. "She'd be happier with just one kid," I said, "if that kid has learned to care about her."

Janice didn't answer so I added, "It might look like the dumb choice, and it sure is the harder choice."

Janice lifted her hands and shook her head. "Ambrose, you old bleeding heart," she said. But she was smiling, real gentle.

"Does this mean I get Society Girl?" asked Ryan.

"If you aren't good to this horse," Janice said, "I'll come and feed you to the grizzly bears." Then she rumpled Ryan's hair and gave him a hug. Right in front of us, Janice actually wrapped her arms around that bratty little kid.

I'd have to tell Mrs. Longhurst what all had happened just because of her horse. Mrs. Longhurst needed to know. And I needed to see the sparkle appear in those glassy blue eyes. It shouldn't be hard to find her. There couldn't be that many seniors' lodges in Edmonton.

As strange as it sounds, Janice realized exactly what I was thinking. Just like best friends might do. "Hey, Ambrose," she said. "I have a feeling you'll be headed for Edmonton the next chance you get. Looking for one special old lady."

I nodded. Janice laughed, watching Mr. Friesen's and Ryan's blank faces.

That's when I decided I'd be the one to

go to the next auction too. I'd take the money Mr. Friesen would pay for Society Girl and I'd find another horse. The last time I hadn't made such a bad choice after all.

This time for sure I'd find a nice young pack horse. And this one I'd be keeping — as sure as my name is Ambrose Virgil Metford.

orca soundings

Orca Soundings is a teen fiction series that features realistic teenage characters in stories that focus on contemporary situations.

Soundings are short, thematic novels ideal for class or independent reading. Written by such stalwart authors as William Bell, Beth Goobie, Sheree Fitch and Kristin Butcher, there will be between eight and ten new titles a year.

For more information and reading copies, please call Orca Book Publishers at 1-800-210-5277.

Other titles in the Orca Soundings series:

Irene Morck was born in St. John, New Brunswick, and grew up on the Canadian prairies. She spent two years in Barbados and ten years in Jamaica, teaching chemistry at a boys' school and doing biochemistry research at the University of the West Indies.

Irene and her husband, Mogens Nielsen, live on a farm near Spruce View, Alberta. They spend as much summer time as possible trail-riding in the mountains. Two of Irene's novels, *Tough Trails* and *Between Brothers*, are trail-riding stories set in the Alberta Rocky Mountains, based on actual events. Society Girl was a real horse that belonged to Mogens. One very hot day, when Society Girl was twenty-five years old, she fell on a steep mountain trail with her pack. That's what gave Irene the idea for *Tough Trails*.

Irene and Mogens enjoy such hobbies as freelance photography, canoeing, cross-country skiing, learning Spanish, and riding and driving their mules and horses.